Usborne
Build your own
MONSTERS
Sticker Book

Designed by Marc Maynard
Written by Simon Tudhope
Illustrated by Gong Studios

Contents

Ravenhold is a land filled with monsters and magic. Many of the most dangerous and powerful monsters are illustrated in this book. Some serve the Shadow Prince, shown on page 16. Others serve no one but themselves. Once you've read about a monster, you can look at the map below to see where it lives.

Lurgur

Deep beneath the fortress of the Shadow Prince, rats scuttle and captives shiver. Lurgur the dungeon-keeper rattles his manacles and snarls: "Quiet now, my little songbirds, or it'll be no slug stew for you!"

Rakunda

Rakunda leads a warrior clan from the eastern wildlands. One of the most fearsome warriors in Ravenhold, he's as fast as a lynx and as strong as ten men.

STATISTICS

- **Strength:** 7
- **Deadliness:** 8
- **Intelligence:** 6
- **Magic force:** 2
- **Realm:** The Urghar Wildlands

3

Maelstrom

The tentacles appear first, snaking above the ship. The lookout cries to the helmsman – but it's already too late! The sailors quake as the ocean seethes, and Maelstrom rises from the deep.

STATISTICS

- Strength: 10
- Deadliness: 7
- Intelligence: 4
- Magic force: 2
- Realm: The Endless Sea

Gorruk

Gorruk follows the herds that migrate across the Khaladz Desert. As the weaker beasts succumb to the scorching sun, she moves in to pick their bones clean.

STATISTICS

- Strength: 7
- Deadliness: 6
- Intelligence: 4
- Magic force: 1
- Realm: The Khaladz Desert

Fengast

In the dark heart of Grimwold Forest, Fengast's victims dangle from the trees. She's wrapped them tight in her unbreakable web – a tasty snack for her ravenous brood!

STATISTICS

- Strength: 6
- Deadliness: 9
- Intelligence: 7
- Magic force: 3
- Realm: Grimwold Forest

Gorm

The Shadow Prince keeps Gorm caged and chained
– but as an army draws near he sets him loose!
Smashing through shields and swatting arrows aside,
Gorm takes out ten men with one swing of his fist.

STATISTICS

- **Strength:** 9
- **Deadliness:** 7
- **Intelligence:** 3
- **Magic force:** 1
- **Realm:** The Dark Mountains

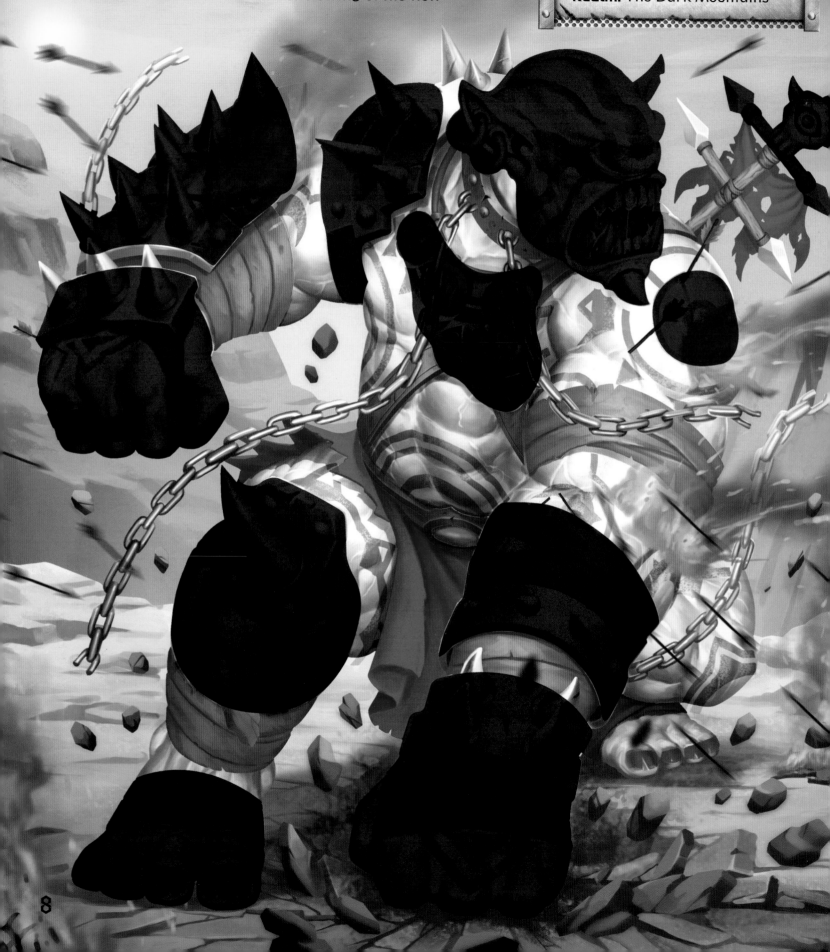

Slaygar

On the wild northern plains, Slaygar leads a raid on a military camp. The soldiers scramble for their weapons – but they're no match for his red-eyed horde! The night soon fills with victorious howls.

STATISTICS

- **Strength:** 7
- **Deadliness:** 8
- **Intelligence:** 7
- **Magic force:** 2
- **Realm:** The Forlorn Plains

Skaluzar

Skalu and Zar were brothers who dared do battle with the Shadow Prince. Defeated and enslaved, they were turned into a double-headed dragon that guards his mountain stronghold.

STATISTICS

- **Strength:** 8
- **Deadliness:** 9
- **Intelligence:** 6
- **Magic force:** 6
- **Realm:** The Dark Mountains

Peeker

Peeker keeps himself to himself, and feeds on birds and bats. But if ever a predator gets too close, his eyes flash red and he opens wide...

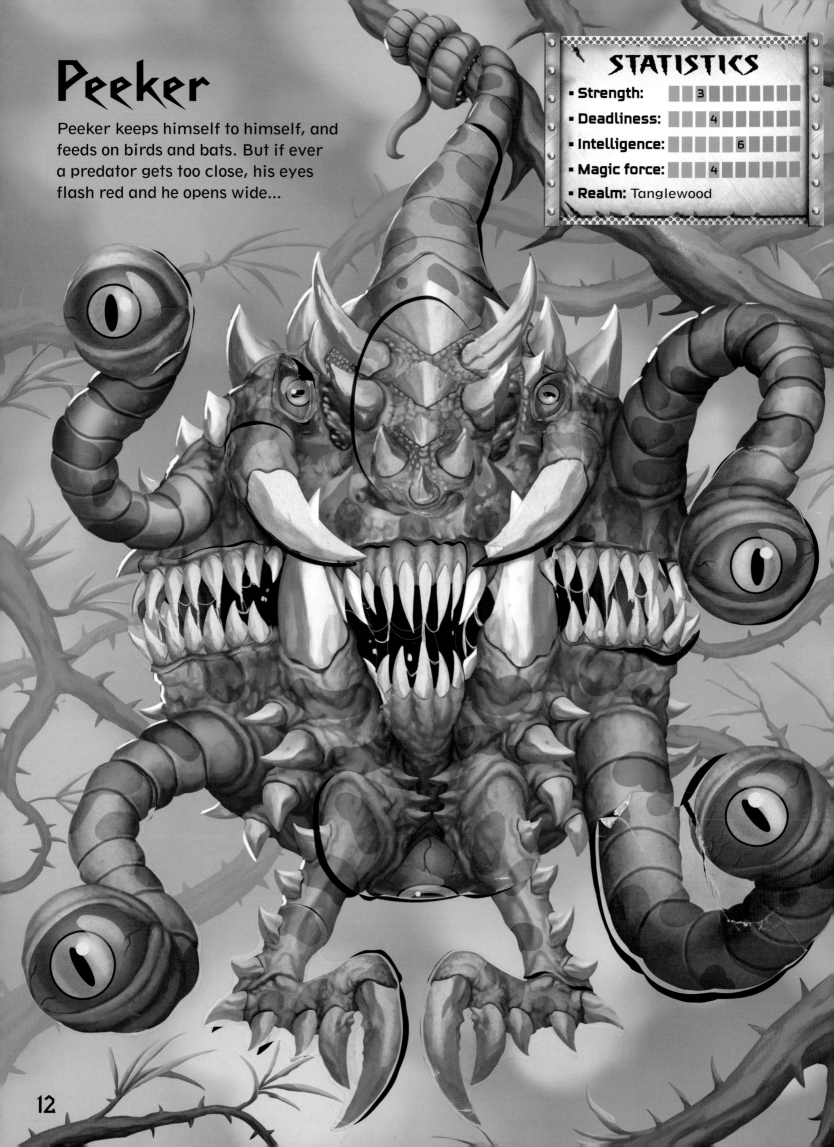

STATISTICS

- **Strength:** 3
- **Deadliness:** 4
- **Intelligence:** 6
- **Magic force:** 4
- **Realm:** Tanglewood

Wretch

Wretch slithers through dark tunnels until she hears footsteps overhead. Then with a piercing screech she bursts through the sand to drag her prey underground.

STATISTICS

- **Strength:** 8
- **Deadliness:** 8
- **Intelligence:** 2
- **Magic force:** 1
- **Realm:** The Shifting Sands

13

Vorghast

Long ago, Vorghast was imprisoned in a lake of fire. As the years went by, his name slowly faded into myth. But now a sorcerer has broken the spell and Vorghast rises again!

STATISTICS

- **Strength:** 8
- **Deadliness:** 10
- **Intelligence:** 7
- **Magic force:** 9
- **Realm:** The Lost Caverns

Asgaroth

Roaming the frozen wastelands of the far north, Asgaroth grabs his enemies with his huge right hand. A deadly cold flows down his arm and turns them slowly to ice. Then – SMASH! – he shatters them with his mace.

STATISTICS

- **Strength:** 7
- **Deadliness:** 6
- **Intelligence:** 6
- **Magic force:** 8
- **Realm:** The Frozen Sea

The Shadow Prince

The Shadow Prince was a sorcerer who found the secret to eternal life. Too late, he learned what that meant! As his body rotted away, his spirit stayed chained to his bones. Cursed to decay but never die, he spreads fear and darkness throughout Ravenhold.

STATISTICS

- Strength: 7
- Deadliness: 8
- Intelligence: 10
- Magic force: 10
- Realm: The Dark Mountains

Mutant

At night, the people of Stonewall hear this strange mutant squelching beneath their streets. Created in an alchemist's laboratory, it escaped to the sewers and survives on insects and rats.

STATISTICS

- **Strength:** 5
- **Deadliness:** 4
- **Intelligence:** 7
- **Magic force:** 4
- **Realm:** Stonewall

Ranghul

High up on the Shadow Prince's fortress, this gigantic gargoyle comes to life. With a blood-curdling shriek it swoops down from its perch to defend the gate from intruders.

STATISTICS

- **Strength:** 8
- **Deadliness:** 7
- **Intelligence:** 3
- **Magic force:** 7
- **Realm:** The Dark Mountains

The Swarm

A deafening drone fills the sky as the people of Stonewall run for cover. And they'd better be quick! This deadly swarm has stingers the size of harpoons and venom that burns right through iron.

STATISTICS

- **Strength:** 5
- **Deadliness:** 9
- **Intelligence:** 4
- **Magic force:** 2
- **Realm:** The Old Mines

Squelch

In the vast southern swamps Squelch lives in his rickety shack. He mutters and murmurs as he waddles along, hunting for flies and raw fish.

Grimsaur

Pirates beware – Grimsaur has a ferocious craving for treasure! Looming up from the depths, she tears whole ships apart in her endless search for more gold.

STATISTICS

- **Strength:** 8
- **Deadliness:** 6
- **Intelligence:** 5
- **Magic force:** 1
- **Realm:** The Emerald Sea

Glossary

- **alchemist:** a type of scientist who tries to transform one substance into another. For example, iron into gold.

- **brood:** the offspring of a spider or insect

- **gargoyle:** a stone carving of a scary creature on the side of a building

- **harpoon:** a big spear with a rope attached. Used for catching large sea creatures.

- **helmsman:** the person who steers a ship

- **horde:** a large group of warriors

- **mace:** a weapon with a spiked metal head attached to a chain or rod

- **manacles:** a metal chain with cuffs at either end to fasten someone's hands or feet together

- **migrate:** travel from one place to live somewhere else

- **mutant:** an animal or person that has transformed into something that looks or behaves differently

- **ravenous:** very hungry

- **sorcerer:** a wizard

- **stronghold:** a castle or fort

- **succumb:** to be defeated by something

- **venom:** poisonous liquid injected by an animal

Edited by Sam Taplin
Additional designs and digital manipulation by Keith Furnival

First published in 2018 by Usborne Publishing Ltd, Usborne House, 83-85 Saffron Hill, London EC1N 8RT, England. www.usborne.com

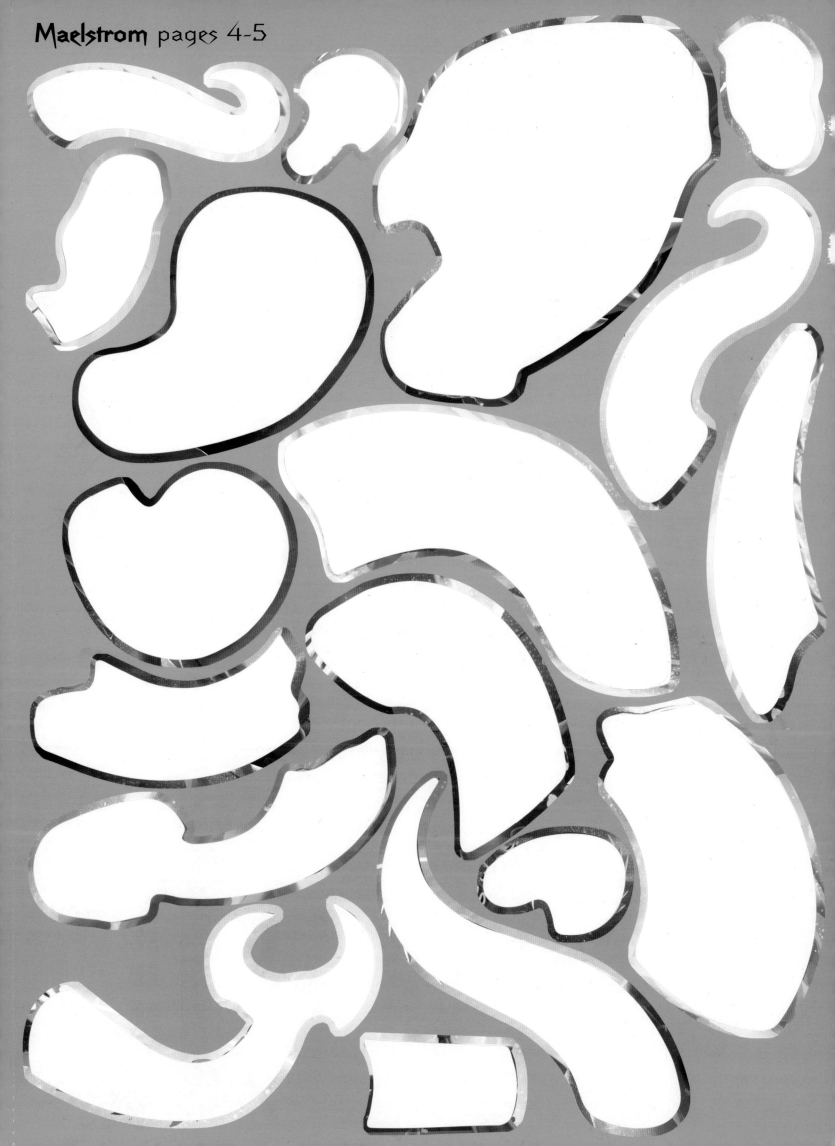

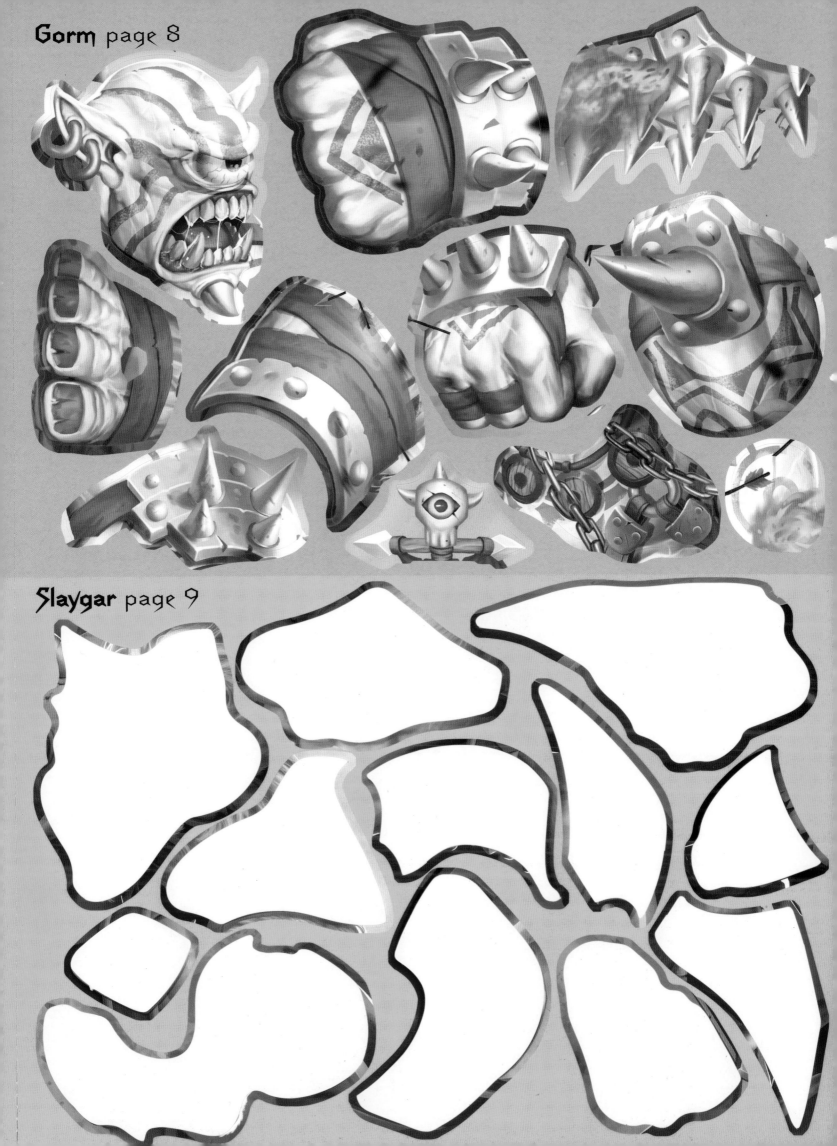

Slaygar page 9

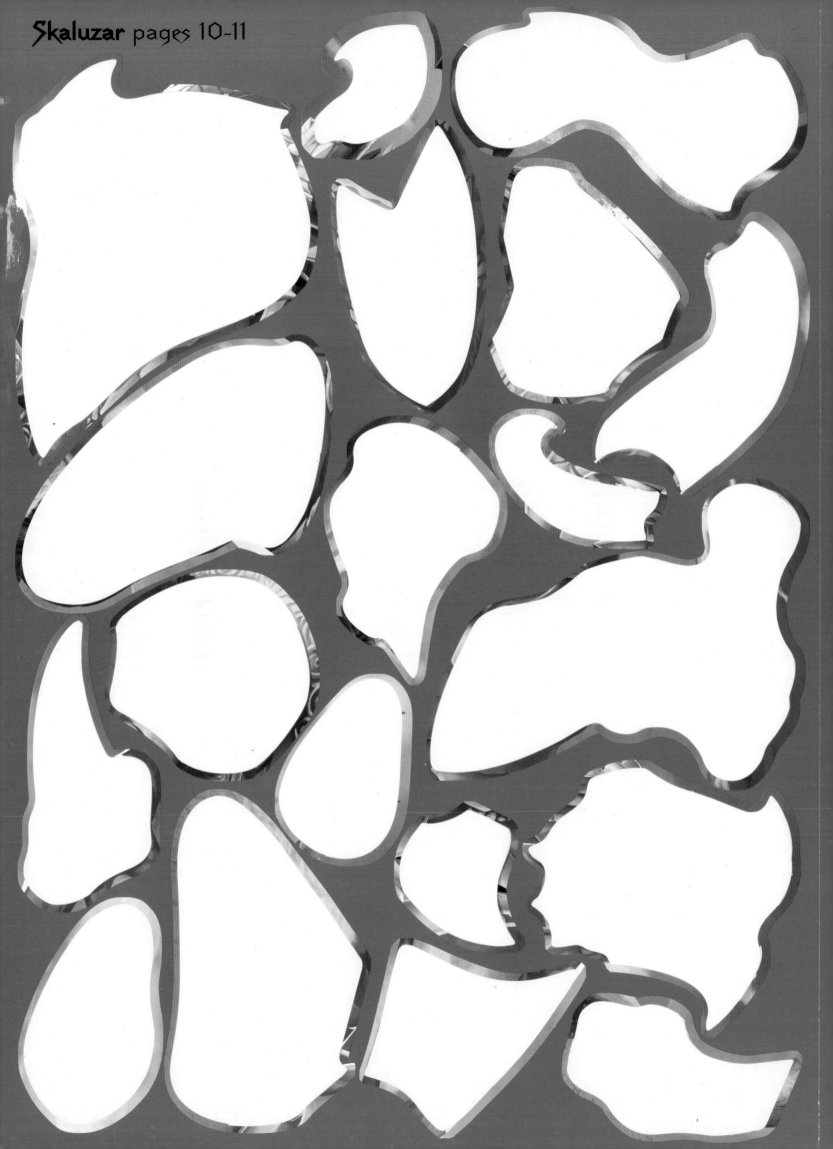

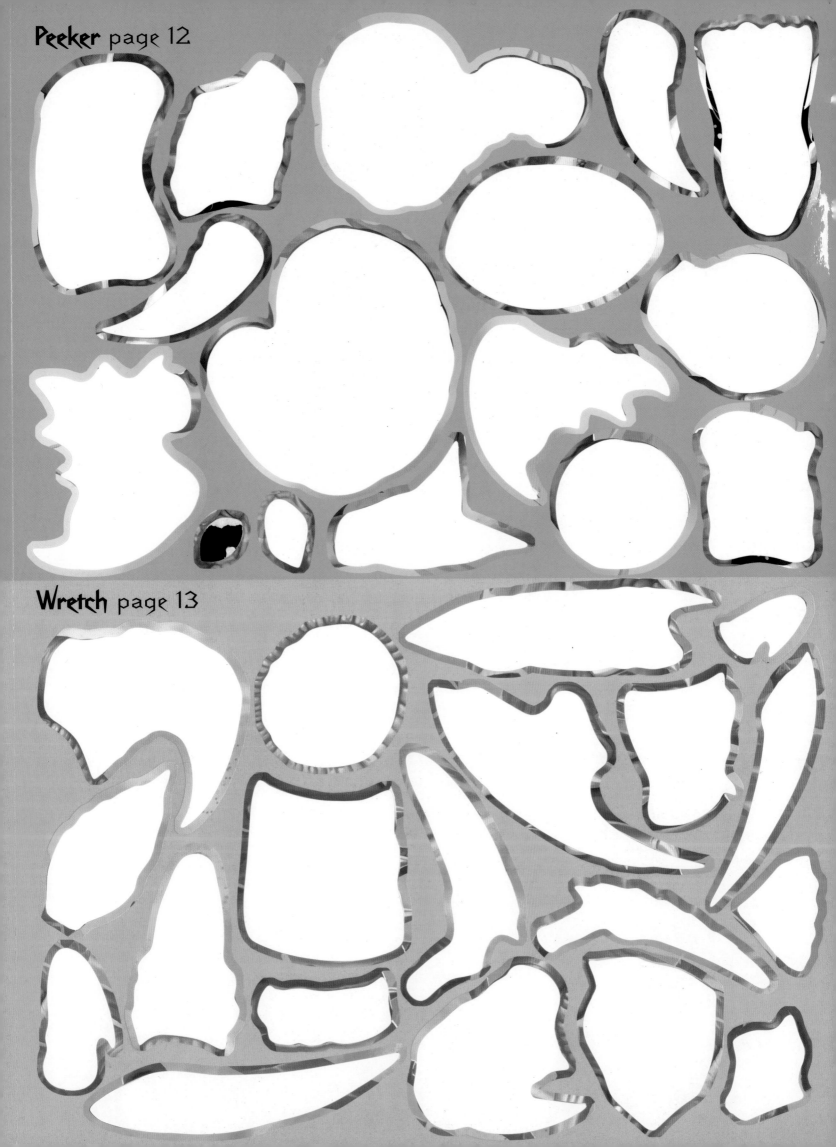

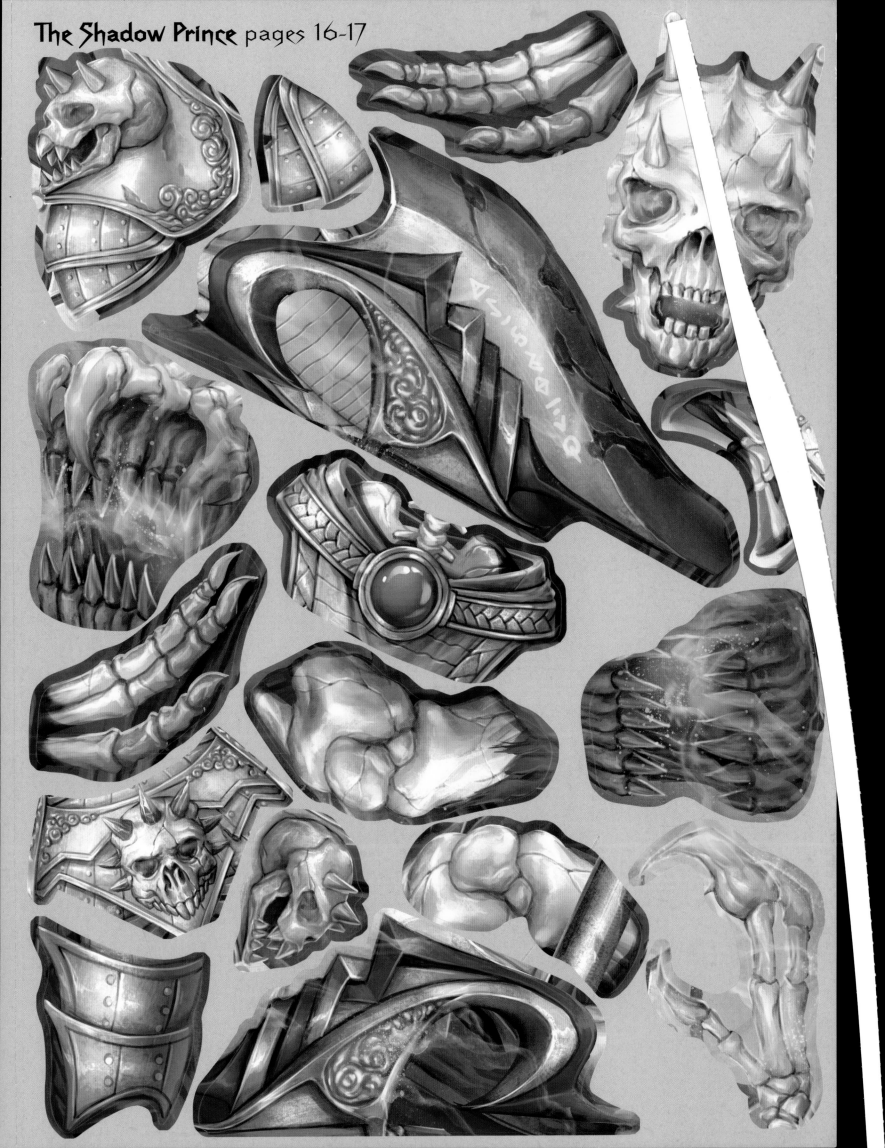